Favorite Pets

Hermit Crabs

by Christina Leaf

BELLWETHER MEDIA • MINNEAPOLIS, MN

Blastoff! Beginners

Blastoff! Beginners are developed by literacy experts and educators to meet the needs of early readers. These engaging informational texts support young children as they begin reading about their world. Through simple language and high frequency words paired with crisp, colorful photos, Blastoff! Beginners launch young readers into the universe of independent reading.

Sight Words in This Book

a	has	not	this
are	here	on	to
be	in	one	which
big	is	the	who
do	it	these	will
eat	like	they	you

This edition first published in 2021 by Bellwether Media, Inc.

No part of this publication may be reproduced in whole or in part without written permission of the publisher. For information regarding permission, write to Bellwether Media, Inc., Attention: Permissions Department, 6012 Blue Circle Drive, Minnetonka, MN 55343.

Library of Congress Cataloging-in-Publication Data

Names: Leaf, Christina, author.
Title: Hermit crabs / by Christina Leaf.
Description: Minneapolis, MN : Bellwether Media, 2021. | Series: Blastoff! beginners: favorite pets | Includes bibliographical references and index. | Audience: Ages PreK-2 | Audience: Grades K-1
Identifiers: LCCN 2020031982 (print) | LCCN 2020031983 (ebook) |
  ISBN 9781644873649 (library binding) | ISBN 9781648340659 (ebook)
Subjects: LCSH: Hermit crabs as pets--Juvenile literature.
Classification: LCC SF459.H47 L43 2021 (print) | LCC SF459.H47 (ebook) | DDC 639/.67--dc23
LC record available at https://lccn.loc.gov/2020031982
LC ebook record available at https://lccn.loc.gov/2020031983
Library of Congress Cataloging-in-Publication Data

Text copyright © 2021 by Bellwether Media, Inc. BLASTOFF! BEGINNERS and associated logos are trademarks and/or registered trademarks of Bellwether Media, Inc.

Editor: Amy McDonald   Designer: Jeffrey Kollock

Printed in the United States of America, North Mankato, MN.

Sep 2021

Table of Contents

Pet Hermit Crabs!	4
Care	8
Life with Hermit Crabs	18
Hermit Crab Facts	22
Glossary	23
To Learn More	24
Index	24

Pet Hermit Crabs!

Who hides in a shell?
A hermit crab!

5

Hermit crabs are fun pets. Which kind do you like?

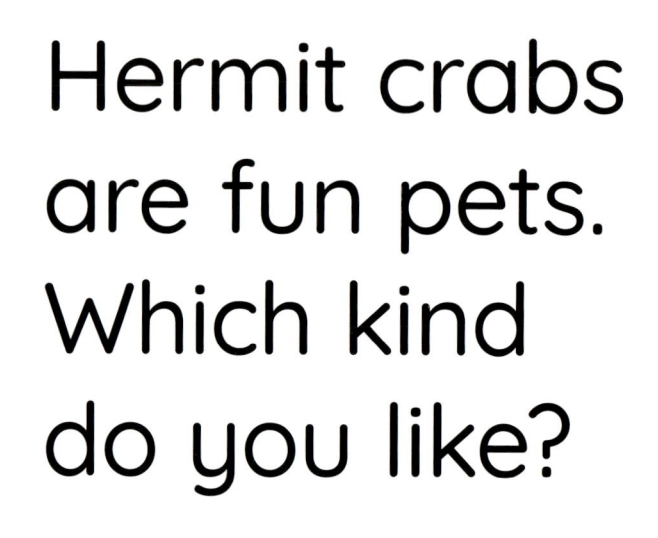

strawberry

Ecuadorian

Caribbean

7

Care

Hermit crabs live in tanks. Sand is on the bottom.

sand

hermit crab tank

They like to be warm. Tanks need **heaters**.

heater

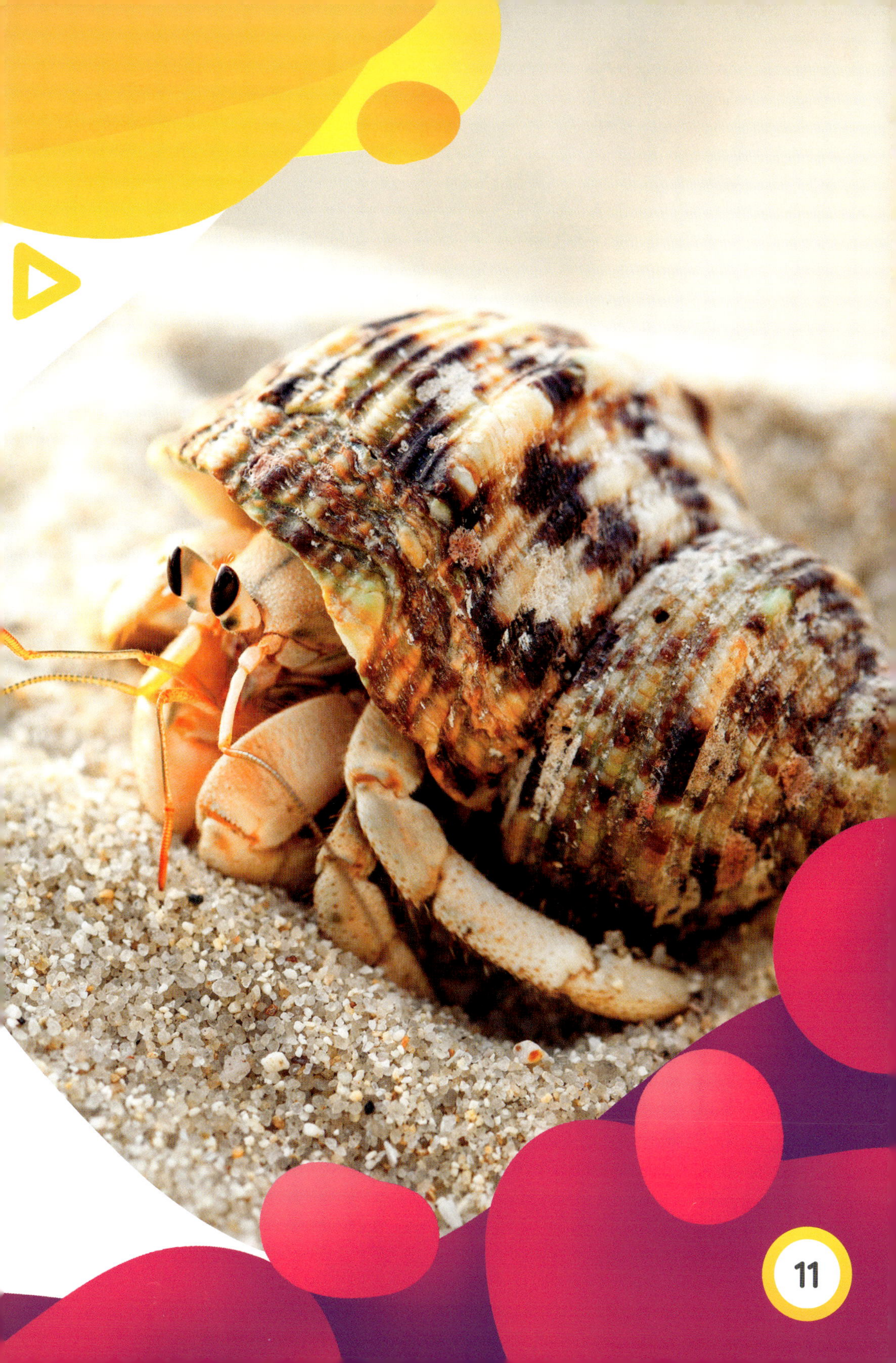

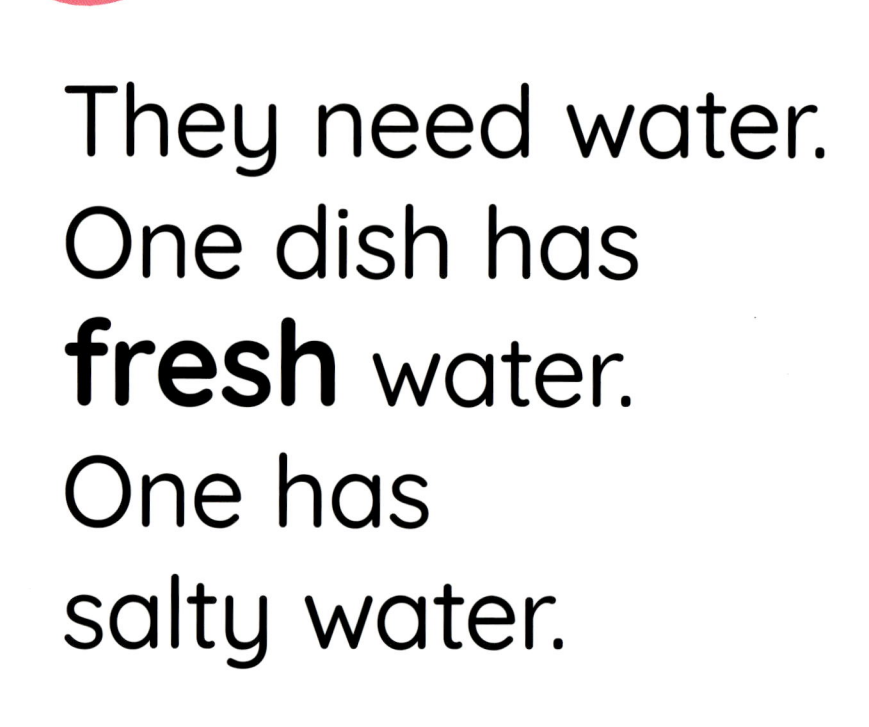

They need water.
One dish has
fresh water.
One has
salty water.

dish

They eat **pellets**. Fruit is a treat!

pellets

fruit ↑

15

These pets need friends. They do not like to be alone.

17

Life with Hermit Crabs

This crab grew big.
It needs
a new shell.

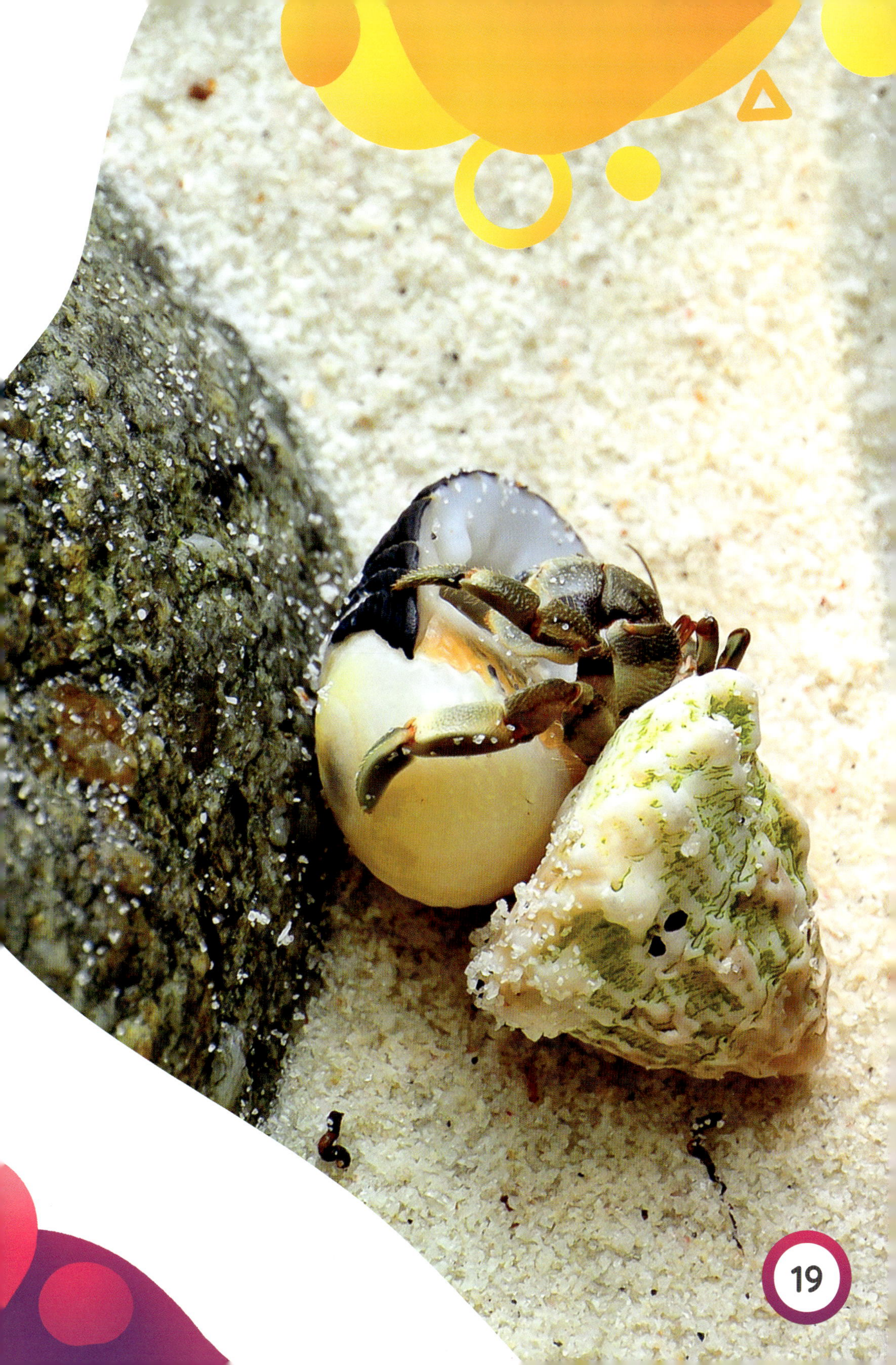

Here are
new shells.
Which will it pick?

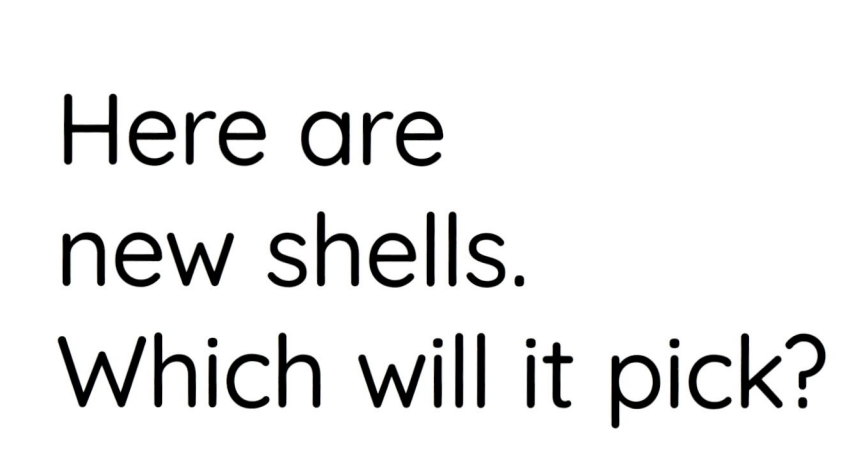

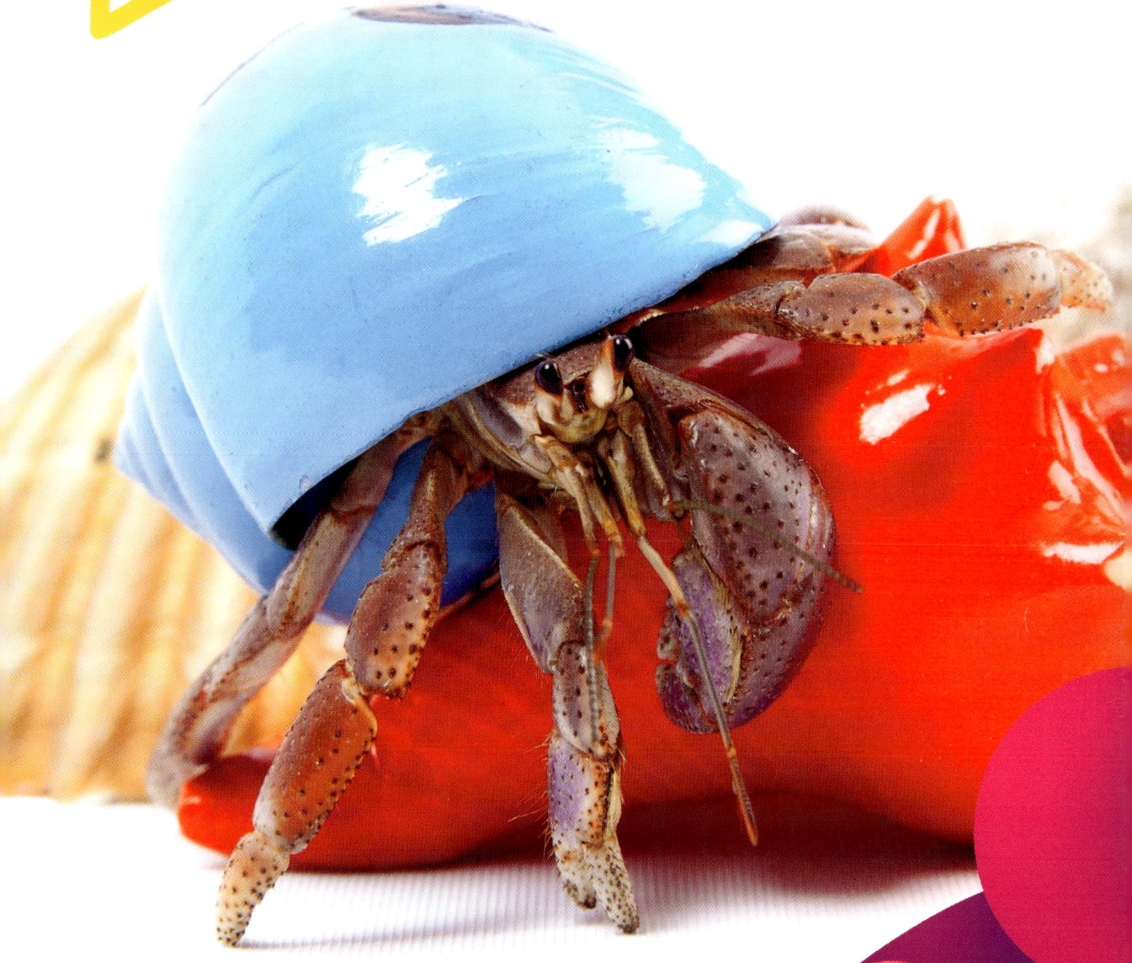

Hermit Crab Facts

Pet Hermit Crab Supplies

- tank
- heater
- two water dishes
- sand

Hermit Crab Needs

a friend | new shells | food

Glossary

fresh
not salty

heaters
tools that give warmth

pellets
small pieces of food

To Learn More

ON THE WEB

FACTSURFER

Factsurfer.com gives you a safe, fun way to find more information.

1. Go to www.factsurfer.com.

2. Enter "pet hermit crabs" into the search box and click 🔍.

3. Select your book cover to see a list of related content.

Index

dish, 12, 13
friends, 16
fruit, 14, 15
grew, 18
heaters, 10
hides, 4
kind, 6
pellets, 14
pick, 20

sand, 8, 9
shell, 4, 18, 20
tanks, 8, 9, 10
warm, 10
water, 12

The images in this book are reproduced through the courtesy of: Eric Isselee, front cover, p. 6; busypix, p. 3; andrewburgess, p. 4; Mirror-Images, pp. 4-5; Zuzha, pp. 6-7; Michiel de Wit, p. 7 (Ecuadorian); Alexander Sviridov, p. 7 (Caribbean); Shatchaya, pp. 8-9; cynoclub, pp. 10, 22 (tank); Chirasak Tolertmongkol/ Alamy, pp. 10-11; Suphatthra olovedog, pp. 12-13; taurus15, p. 14; Natalia Harper/ Alamy, pp. 14-15; JetKat, pp. 16-17; DangBen, pp. 18-19; mary981, pp. 20-21; Sirichai Puangsuwan, p. 20; givaga, pp. 20-21; Pornpoj Phongpatimeth, p. 22 (dish); Raihana Asral, p. 22 (dish); kasarp studio, p. 22 (friend); jiraphoto, p. 22 (shells); Thummasorn Moongfaidee, p. 22 (food); Farion_O, p. 23 (fresh); Juniors Bildarchiv/ Alamy, p. 23 (heater); Logo Mimi, p. 23 (pellets).